James and the Pixie

Januarius

A CIP catalogue record for this title is available from the British Library.

ISBN 9781784555382 (paperback)
ISBN 9781784555405 (hardback)

www.austinmacauley.com

First Published (2015)
Austin Macauley Publishers Ltd.
25 Canada Square
Canary Wharf
London
E14 5LB

Printed and bound in Great Britain

Dedicated to young people everywhere who take delight in the everyday joy of the magic of childhood.

One

James, who had just had his sixth birthday, was feeling bored. His parents had just moved into a big old country house and he had left all his friends behind in London. He wasn't much looking forward to starting his new school at the end of the summer holidays.

'James,' said his mother as he was finishing his breakfast, 'why don't you go outside and explore the garden?'

'Alright mother,' he replied.

It was a glorious hot day in the middle of August. The birds were singing and the bees were buzzing happily to themselves, collecting the nectar from the multitude of flowers all around him. The sumptuous summer smells were captivating.

He had never been in a real garden before coming to the country as they had lived in a flat in London surrounded by buildings. James was astonished by the huge variety of plants and flowers. There was even a pool with brightly coloured fish and a frog or two. Right at the bottom of the garden, beside a broken down fence, was a huge old mulberry tree. James didn't know it was a mulberry tree, or that mulberry trees were the favourite homes for the little people, sometimes called pixies or elves.

He was instantly attracted to the tree because, having many low braches, it looked fairly easy to climb. He immediately ran down the garden, caught hold of one and started swinging on it.

'Hi! Watch out!' called a voice.

James stopped swinging for a moment, stood up and looked around. Then, not seeing anyone, he started swinging again. '

'Stop it!' called the voice again, this time considerably more agitated.

James dropped to the ground once more and shouted - 'But who's there?'

'I'll tell you who's there,' answered the voice. Then to his amazement a small man popped out of a hole in the tree trunk.

He was about half a metre tall and had a large friendly face, albeit looking a bit cross, with a red nose and a short trim beard. He was dressed all in green with a pointed hat, and a brown belt around his middle which had a big brass buckle in the middle.

'Surely you know that this is a mulberry tree,' he said, 'and in nearly every mulberry tree you will find a pixie living.'

'No,' answered a bewildered James, 'I didn't know that.'

'Goodness me,' replied the pixie. 'What is the world coming to? Well you know now as this is one and it is also my home, or what's left of it since you've nearly shaken it all to bits!'

'Oh I'm truly sorry,' said James apologetically. 'I promise that I won't do it again.' The pixie looked at James and smiled and said' 'Very well then, but you can come and help me clean up the mess.'

'But how can I do that' asked James, I'm much too big to squeeze into that small hole otherwise I'd be only too pleased to.'

'That is what you think,' laughed the pixie. 'Why do you think that we pixies choose to live in mulberry trees?' he asked.

'I've no idea,' replied James, intrigued to know the answer.

'Well it's because of their magical properties' continued the pixie.

'Come here,' he beckoned, 'and I will tell you a big secret.'

He pulled off a mulberry leaf and gave it to his excited young friend.

'Now, rub it between your fingers and make a wish and you can be any size that you like, but only for about 15 minutes or so. Then the magic starts to wear off, but it will be long enough for you to come and help me tidy up.'

4

James did as he was told and wished to be half his size. In an instant he shrunk to being less than half a metre tall and had clambered up the tree trunk. He followed the pixie into the hole and through a maze of passages untill he arrived in a splendid room with furniture strewn all over the place.

Together they worked and in no time at all the table and chairs had all been put back into their rightful places. The grandfather clock stood proudly in the corner and a fire blazed cheerfully in the grate.

'It's not an ordinary fire,' the pixie explained, 'but part of the mystical wonder of the mulberry tree. It generates a very special source of energy which gives it its strange magical powers. By the way, my name is William.'

'And mine is James,' he replied. Then they shook hands and a splendid friendship was started.

James suddenly felt himself starting to grow again.

'I think that I should be going,' he said to William. Then he made his way as quickly as he could down the passages to the hole in the trunk where he had first met his friend. Back in the sunshine he soon returned to his old size again.

'Whew,' he thought, 'only just in time.'

'Goodbye William!' he called.

'Goodbye James,' came the reply from deep within the tree. 'Remember though, the magic only works once a day and if you tell anyone about it, it will stop altogether.'

'James!' called a voice. It was his mother. 'Have you had a nice play in the garden?'

'Lovely,' replied her smiling son.

Two

The following morning it was raining and James had to stay indoors, spending most of the time sitting on the edge of his bed looking out of his bedroom window towards the bottom of the garden. He was hoping to catch a glimpse of his new found friend. He closed his eyes for a moment and was just beginning to think that he must have dreamed it all when he heard a cough behind him.

He looked around and there to his astonishment was William, who had suddenly appeared as if from nowhere.

'How did you get there?' he asked.

'It's easy' replied William, 'I've got underground passages all over the place.'

'Oh, will you show me?' pleaded James, jumping up and sitting next to him.

'Of course,' came the reply, 'but first there is something I want you to do.

'What's that?' asked James, intrigued beyond measure.

'Well you see,' continued William, 'We pixies have a special vocation in life which is to see that all the plants and animals are looked after and happy, because they in turn make the world such a wonderful place for everyone to live in.'

'So what is this job?' asked James.

'Well, earlier this morning Mrs Rabbit told her twins to stay indoors because it was raining, but while she was looking after her new baby they slipped out to play with their friends and now they are nowhere to be seen. She came to me asking if I could assist in finding them. This is where your help could be invaluable.'

'Right,' said James. 'Where do we start looking?'

'Follow me,' replied the little man.

He walked over to the fireplace which was surrounded by large oak panels. Then, in front of his excited young friend, he slid one of them to the left revealing an old stone staircase and started descending.

'Hold on a minute,' yelled James, going over to his toy box to collect his torch. In a trice he bounded across the room and was soon following him down the steps and into a rather gloomy passageway.

'Oh, I forgot that humans can't see in the dark,' said William. 'Now follow me closely.'

Soon they were in a long, damp tunnel and James was glad that he had remembered his torch. He was just starting to become a little frightened when he noticed a small pinprick of light that was getting brighter by the second. Then something startled him.

'What's that funny noise?' he inquired.

'You just wait and see,' chuckled his friend as they trudged towards it.

Suddenly they emerged into sunlight and James thought that there must have been a cloud burst. But he could not understand why they were not getting wet. It was then that he realised that they were standing underneath a waterfall.

'How exhilarating,' he thought.

'Now be very careful as it's rather slippery,' warned William.

James did as he was told and soon they were standing in bright sunshine by the side of a river into which the waterfall was plunging. It had stopped raining, and the river banks were radiant with rainbows as the hot sun evaporated the dampness everywhere.

'Now, the worrying thing is...' said William. 'This is where the twins usually play.' 'Hold on, I think that I can hear something' interrupted his young friend.

Sure enough there were faint calls of help wafting towards them from down the stream somewhere.

'Come on!' he urged, running like mad along the bank towards the ever more desperate cries. Soon they saw the twin bunnies in a small boat going round and round on the edge of what appeared to be a whirlpool.

'Quick!' he shouted to William, 'do you have a Mulberry leaf?'

'Of course,' he answered, immediately placing a piece into James' hand as the boat was being sucked ever faster and faster towards the centre of the whirlpool. The distressed crying of the twins was becoming ever more frantic.

'I wish that I was a giant,' wished James, rubbing the leaf frantically between his fingers and in an instant he was ten metres tall. Then just as the tiny boat was about to be sucked under, he leaned across the river and plucked the two little bunnies out of the boat to safety.

'Phew, that was close' he gasped, but William was too busy telling those naughty twins how thoughtless and silly they had been in disobeying their mother. He made them promise never to do so again.

As William took them back home, James waited until he had regained his proper size again before retracing his steps back home to his bedroom, where he shut the fireside panel and lay back on his bed, exhausted.

'My' he thought, 'what an adventure I've had.'

Three

It had been a miserable couple of days and James had just returned from visiting his cousin Gerald who lived just a few miles away. He had so badly wanted to tell him about William and the mulberry tree with its magical properties, and the adventures that he had enjoyed since moving into his new home, but he knew that if he did so all of the trees magic would disappear just as William had warned him. So he had said nothing.

As soon as he was out of the car he ran around to the back of the house.

'Don't be too long,' shouted his mother as he disappeared down the garden. 'It will soon be tea time.'

'All right,' came his reply.

He arrived at the mulberry tree excited and out of breath.

'William!' he called, but there was no reply,.

James climbed up to the hole in the trunk and called again, this time much louder.

'All right all Right' snapped an agitated voice beside him, 'there's no need to deafen me.'

'I'm sorry,' apologised James, 'but I was worried that I was going to miss you. 'I've been visiting my cousin Gerald for a couple of days' he continued, 'and I've only just got back.'

'Well, I'm pleased to see you,' said William, 'because a most extraordinary thing has occurred and there really is no accounting for it whatsoever.'

'What's happened?' asked his curious friend.

'Well you'd better come and see for yourself,' came the concerned reply.

James followed him down the garden to the pond which was nearly all dried up. The fish and the frogs were looking very sorry for themselves indeed.

'If only we could understand what they were saying,' said James, more than a little worried, 'then maybe they could tell us what has happened.'

'Well, if you squeeze the juice of a ripe mulberry on to your thumb and hold it close to your ear, you will be able to understand them,' advised William. 'The problem is that I have already had to use one earlier, as Mrs thrush needed some help if finding one of her newly fledged chicks and as you know you only get one chance every day to use the trees magical powers so I have been unable to talk to them.'

James ran back to the Mulberry tree and did as his friend suggested, then returning to the pond he lifted his thumb to his ear and sure enough he could hear the big Red Carp saying that the pond had developed a leak underneath one of its large stones and all the water was gradually seeping out. James told William and together they waded into the now shallow pond and James asked the Carp which of the large stones it was. 'Right here, beneath this one' it answered, swimming towards the biggest one.

Then with William's help, together they pulled it back and saw the hole. It was about the size of a tennis ball and they could hear the water gurgling as it slowly drained away. In a moment James was off like a shot to the toy box in his bedroom and reappeared a minute or so later with his brand new cricket ball.

Then, pushing it into the crevice, where it fitted as snuggly as a bath plug, he and William replaced the stone and waited. Then to everyone's delight the pond slowly started to fill up again.

'Oh thank you,' said the grateful carp.

'Yes, thank you,' croacked the frogs.

'Well done,' said William, but James was nowhere to be seen. He had spotted his mother coming and had run off meet her.

'You look excited,' she said.

'Well it's been an exciting few minutes,' he replied with a twinkle in his eye.

Four

James was feeling totally miserable, He had been out since the early morning with his mother visiting the local vicar and going round the shops. All he really wanted was to see what William was up to. At long last they arrived home and straight away he ran to the bottom of the garden.

'William!' he called, but there was no reply.

'William!' he called again, this time as loudly as he could, but still no one answered him. Suddenly he saw a friendly squirrel sitting in the branches of the mulberry tree, who was obviously trying to tell him something.

So James, finding the biggest mulberry that he could, picked it and squeezed the juice on to his thumb and put his hand up to his ear.

'William has fallen down and hurt himself!' said the Squirrel.

'Where about is he?' asked an extremely concerned James.

'Just follow me' came the reply.

Jumping over the gate in the middle of the old garden fence, the squirrel started running towards the canal which was about half a mile away. James grabbed a mulberry leaf, and, quick as a flash, ran after his new little friend. After a few minutes they arrived at the canal bank and there, to James' horror, in the middle of the tow path he saw William's hat. He picked it up just as a barge, which had been stationary nearby, started to move off. It was being towed along by a big brown shire horse.

As it passed them James was sure he caught a glimpse of his little friend all tied up inside the cabin.

Realising the danger he was in, together they ran down the tow path as fast as they could and reached an approaching lock a good two minutes before the barge came into sight again.

There they hid behind a bush until it arrived. Then, as the bargeman was operating the sluice gates, James took a piece of mulberry leaf and rubbed it between his fingers. He wished to be as small as a mouse before climbing onto the squirrel's back.

They then scampered over to the barge, jumped on to its deck and disappeared into the cabin through its open door.

There they found William, who was so pleased to see them that he nearly shouted out and gave the whole game away. But instead, he gestured to his animal friend to bite through his bonds. He immediately did, and in no time at all William was free again.

'Here,' said James, giving him the rest of the mulberry leaf, 'make yourself as small as a mouse.'

Then, as the magic worked, he also climbed up and joined James on the squirrel's back. Then scampering through the cabin door, they sped across the barge's deck, leapt on to the tow path like jockeys in the Grand National and then galloped towards home.

'Hi stop, stop,' shouted the gypsy bargeman, but the squirrel was far too nimble. In the twinkling of an eye the three friends disappeared into the thick wooded undergrowth. In a few minutes they were safely back home.

'Phew,' gasped James as he started to resume his usual height. 'Now that was a near thing.

'Thank you both,' said William, smiling happily at them but still rubbing his sore knee.

'Well it is this very brave Squirrel that we really need to thank,' concluded James.

Five

It was early on a summer evening during the school holidays and James had been visiting his cousin Gerald. It had been a wonderfully hot day and he had been enchanted watching the swallows swooping down above the trees and listening to a cuckoo. They'd spent hours playing together in the woods close to where he lived and James had arrived back home tired but happy.

He had desperately wanted to tell Gerald about William his pixie friend and the magical mulberry tree at the bottom of the garden where he lived and his fantastic adventures, but he decided not to. What if all the mulberry trees magic really did disappear, as William had warned would happen if he told anybody about it?

As soon as he was back home he got out of the car, and ran down the garden as fast as he could in the hope of seeing William.

'Don't be long James!' called his Mother after him. 'It's nearly supper time.'

'Oh I'm so glad to see you,' said William, who was just stepping out of the hole in the mulberry tree as his young friend arrived. 'I have just come across a very mysterious door which I can't open and I was hoping that you would be able to help me.'

'Of course' replied James almost bubbling over with curiosity. 'Where is it?'

'Well, if you come with me I will show you' came the answer.

William made his way to the back of the mulberry tree and started climbing up on the lower branches. James followed him closely and there, about half way up in its trunk and only just visible, was a small door that was quite impossible to see from the ground.

'Is this it?' asked James.

'Yes' replied William.

'How did you come to find it?' asked his friend.

'Well this part of the trunk had always been covered with moss and I only discovered it this afternoon when I was cleaning it and giving the bark a bit of a polish. I don't know what is behind it but I'm pretty sure that it will be something very exciting,' answered William.

'Well what do you think that we might find?' asked James.

'There's only one way to find out,' replied William, 'and that is to open it, but at the moment it is stuck fast.'

So together the two friends tugged and pulled, but no matter how hard they tried it wouldn't budge and remained shut, as solid as a rock. '

Bother' exclaimed William.

'Wait a minute' said James, I've got a terrific idea.'

He climbed down and ran towards his father's garden shed, emerging a few moments later with a long coil of rope. Returning to his friend, he quickly tied one end of the rope around the door handle and lowered the other to the ground.

'Now, if we both get down and make ourselves taller, we should be able to pull it open.'

'What a great idea' enthused William.

This they did and straight away started rubbing a magic mulberry leaf between their fingers while wishing to be three metres tall. Almost immediately they started to grow and were soon standing looking straight down at the old stubborn door.

Like a tug of war team, they pulled on the rope as hard as they could. Suddenly, with a loud bang it burst open, leaving the two friends, who had fallen backwards on to the lawn, spread-eagled on the ground.

'Hooray!' cheered James.

'Bravo!' added William. Then, sitting up, they waited until they had regained their proper size, before climbing back to satisfy their curiosity. Just at that moment James' mother called telling him it was time for supper.

'Oh what a nuisance,' he exclaimed.

'Never mind,' commiserated his friend gently closing the door again. 'We will explore inside together tomorrow.'

James untied the rope from the door handle and reluctantly climbed down and returned it to the garden shed, then running back home entered the dining room just as his father returned from work.

'Have you had an exciting day James?' he asked.

'Oh lovely Daddy,' he replied and told him about all the games that he had played with Gerald in the woods.

'I'm so glad,' said his Father, adding, 'now you go and wash your hands and get ready for supper, there's a good boy.'

James did as he was told and soon the three of them were sat at the table having a meal together.

'How about if it is a nice day tomorrow that we all go fishing?' asked his father, smiling happily.

'Oh yes please,' answered his excited son.

'What a splendid idea,' added his Mother. 'I shall make a picnic for us all.'

Six

The following morning James was up with the Lark and hastily getting dressed. He rushed downstairs and dashed up the garden before having breakfast to see William. He couldn't wait to find out what was behind the old door in the mulberry tree.

It was a slightly misty start to the day but every minute was getting warmer, as the sun appeared like a ball of orange gold through the leaves of the mulberry tree.

'William!' he called, but not too loudly, so as not to wake his parents. After a minute or so his pixie friend appeared, grumpily rubbing his eyes at being so rudely awakened.

'My, you're up early!' he complained.

'I know,' said James excitedly. 'I couldn't sleep and was longing to see what was behind that door.'

'All right,' said his friend with a yawn, 'but wait until I get my climbing boots on and I'll be with you.'

With that he disappeared into the mulberry tree, reappearing a few minutes later wearing them and looking his old cheerful self again. Then together they made their way around to the back of the tree. Soon they reached a small wooden platform that William had erected while James was in bed. Standing on it gingerly, they opened the mysterious door.

James could scarcely contain his excitement as together they peered inside. At first they could see nothing as it took a little while for their eyes to get used to its gloomy interior.

Then eventually, as they became accustomed to the dark, they saw what appeared to be dozens of small mushrooms growing all over the floor of what was in fact a small room.

They were all glowing, covered as they were in either a gold or silver sheen. The gold with light blue stalks while the silver had red.

'What do you think that they are?' asked James.

'This is so extraordinary,' replied William. 'I knew that they used to exist, but I never thought to ever see one as my uncle Sylvester told me that they had long ago become extinct.'

'Oh do tell me' pleaded James.

'I will do better than that' came the answer. Then, picking one of each colour and closing the door he started to climb down. James quickly followed him and when they were safely on the ground William broke off a small piece of the gold mushroom with the blue stalk and gave it to his friend.

'Here, taste this,' he urged.

James did so, and suddenly he felt strange, as if he was floating on air. Looking down he realised that he was in fact walking on air a few centimetres above Williams' head.

'Hey get me down!' he shouted to his friend.

'Here, catch!' said his pixie friend, laughing, and threw him a tiny piece of the silver mushroom. James caught it and almost in a panic put it in his mouth. To his relief he slowly glided to the ground.

'Wow, how did that happen?' he asked.

'Well' replied William. 'These are the legendry Camelot mushrooms that Merlin, King Arthur's wizard cultivated. Thousands of years ago, very early in the history of England there was a King whose name was Arthur and his advisor was a Magician named Merlin. One day, when they were walking in Wiltshire they came across a piece of land and felt a very powerful source of healing energy, just like the Tor hill in Glastonbury.

On that he had placed a stone monument so that his people would know where to go to be healed when they were ill. This was many years before there were such people as doctors. When he felt this new amazing surge of healing power he asked Merlin to build a big round stone circle so that his people from the south of England would know where to come to be made better when they were poorly. The problem was that there weren't any large stones locally and the nearest were 160 miles away in Wales. They were much too far away and heavy to be carried. So Merlin, using his most powerful magic created these mushrooms which, once placed underneath the huge stones, made them float up so that it was easy to push them all the way to what is now called Stonehenge.'

'Goodness me,' said James. Are these exactly the same as the mushrooms Merlin made?'

'Well my uncle Sylvester described them as being much bigger but we shall see,' smiled his friend.

'Now remember, the more you bite off the gold one the higher it will lift you and you need exactly the same amount of the silver one to return you back to earth, but the thing is, I don't know how long each mushroom's magic lasts so you must use them very carefully.'

Just then James' Mother came out into the garden.

'It's time for breakfast James,' she called.

'Goodbye William,' said James putting the precious fungi into his pocket.

'Goodbye' answered his friend from the middle of the tree. He had already disappeared.

Seven

As soon as breakfast was finished James helped his father load the picnic basket into the car with three deck chairs, a blanket, a couple of towels and his bucket and spade, while his mother finished tidying up.

Then, leaving everything spick and span, his father looked up and they were off. As a special treat he had decided to take them to the seaside, about half an hour's drive away.

They arrived, parked the car and set off.

James of course was thrilled. He had never been to the sea-side before. After making several sand castles with turrets and flags on the top he joined in with lots of games with the other children, who were playing around the water's edge.

His parents meanwhile lay back in their deck chairs and enjoyed the sunshine while listening to the gulls and the sea gently lapping on the shore. After a couple of hours his mother opened the picnic basket and handed out the sandwiches and lemonade and the three of them tucked in ravenously. Then his father decided that it was time to fish.

Closing the hamper they carried everything back to the car and set off for the pier where he hired a boat for the afternoon complete with fishing tackle. Soon, having rowed about 30 metres from the shore, they started to fish. After about 20 minutes James was becoming a bit frustrated as at no time did he get a bite.

His mother, however, had soon caught a small mackerel and laughed out loud as it wriggled on the deck of the boat as she landed it.

'Well done my dear,' said his father.

However, it looked so sad flipping about that she decided to put it back in the sea where they watched it swim happily away. The beach was filled with holiday makers, but the biggest crowd was around the ice cream stall.

'Daddy,' asked James, 'could we have an ice cream?'

'What a lovely idea,' said his mother, and opening her bag, she took out some money and gave it to him to pay for them while his father rowed the boat towards the shore. James jumped out and ran off in the direction of the stall.

'Three choc-ices would be nice,' called his mother after him as he disappeared from view.

While James waited, he looked across at the tall cliffs on the other side of a peninsular jutting out towards the sea. He saw what he thought was a small girl stuck halfway up the cliff face waving frantically!

Forgetting everything, he ran as fast as he could around the bay and was soon standing right underneath her.

When he arrived, he could see that other people were also making their way quickly towards the same spot so he immediately reached for the gold mushroom that William had given him and took a small bite. Straight away he started to float up towards her, keeping as close to the side of the cliff as possible whilst trying to make it look as if he was climbing.

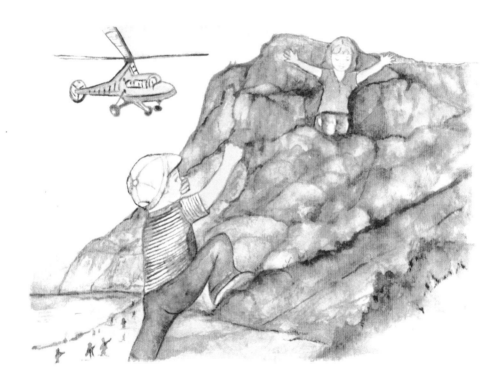

After a third nibble of the mushroom, he was right underneath her. Then she slipped!

She would have fallen had James not have grabbed hold of her as tightly as he could.

'It's all right,' he comforted as she cried out loud. 'Just you hold on to me and whatever you do, don't look down.'

Then, reaching for the silver mushroom and again trying to make it look as if he was climbing, he took a big bite and together they floated slowly down the cliff face to safety.

By the time they had arrived at the bottom a large crowd of onlookers had gathered who clapped and cheered while others took photographs. Just at that very moment the little girl's parents came running around the peninsular, overjoyed at seeing her safe and unharmed.

'Who rescued you?' they asked, but her reply was drowned out as a large helicopter arrived and landed close by. The pilots quickly jumped down, wanting to know what had happened and who had phoned for their help.

'It was me,' replied the girl's father. 'We were walking along the cliff path when suddenly part of it gave way and there was a bit of a landslide and our little girl, who was walking slightly ahead slipped and slid down on to a ledge half way up the cliff.'

'Well how did she get down?' asked the senior pilot, taking out his notebook to make a record of what was being said.

'Well a little boy climbed up and saved her,' came a chorus of replies.

'Goodness me!' he replied. 'That was very brave of him. Where is he?'

James however was nowhere to be seen. In the middle of all the commotion he had vanished and was soon standing in the centre of the crowd of people around the ice cream stall. A few minutes later he was back in the boat with his parents fishing again when his mother asked;

'What was all that noise about?'

'A little girl was stuck up that cliff,' he replied, pointing in the direction of the peninsular. 'She was rescued. It was very exciting.'

Just at that moment his father felt a big bite on the end of his fishing line. It was another mackeral. They let it go and watched it swim away in the glittering water.

Upon returning home, James rushed up the garden to see his pixie friend, as he couldn't wait to tell him about his adventure at the seaside.

'Well you were very brave,' said William. 'I think that King Arthur and Merlin would have been extremely proud of you.'

Eight

The following morning, after the excitement of the previous day, James was up a little later than usual and arrived downstairs just as his mother was preparing the breakfast.

'Why don't you go and play in the garden for a little while and I'll call you when it's ready?' she said.

James did as she asked and straight away went up to see William who was standing at the bottom of the mulberry tree looking very excited indeed.

'Hello James,' he said, and before his young friend could reply added, 'I've just received some great news.'

'Oh do tell me,' he enquired, his curiosity almost at breaking point.

'Well,' continued William, 'every morning we pixies cast runes.'

'What are they?' asked James as William took some very strange looking stones out of his pocket.

'Well he added, you humans keep in touch with each other in all sorts of ways, like the telephone and radio and television and newspapers, but for thousands of years we pixies have done so by casting the runes. These are Runes,' he said, showing them to his little friend. 'We throw them on to the floor in a special way. That is called casting them. When they land, according to the shapes that they form, they reveal messages from other pixies and tell us what is going to happen during the day. They are a bit like your computers as their energy is all inter-connected, so in this way we can talk to each other all over the country.'

'So what did they say this morning?' asked James.

'Well I'll show you,' he replied, casting them on to the ground where they formed a double star shape.

'There,' said William. 'What do you see?'

'They have formed into two stars,' came the reply.

'And that can only mean one thing,' said William triumphantly.

'Oh do tell me,' said James.

'It means' replied his pixie friend, that Gywn ap Nudd, the Fairy King is going send Titania the Fairy Queen to visit me today.

'Oh, might it be possible for me to see her?' asked his eager friend.

But before William could reply his mother called up the garden to tell him that his breakfast was ready. In a flash, William had disappeared into the mulberry tree.

'James,' said his mother as he was finishing his breakfast, 'You know that you start your new school next week?'

'Yes Mother,' answered James.

'Well we need to go into town today to get you your new uniform.'

'Oh dear' replied her anguished son. 'Must we go today?'

'Yes, I'm afraid we must,' she said. 'I have arranged for you to be measured up just in case there are alterations to be made, and they could well take a whole week.'

The rest of the morning was spent traipsing around the shops getting everything that he would need to start at his new school so that he would be, as his mother said, a credit to his family.

'Why are you looking so miserable?' she asked, as he tried on his new blazer. 'You do want to look smart don't you?'

'Yes Mother' he replied, 'but it is such a lovely day for playing outside.'

'Never mind dear,' she said, 'you will have all this afternoon to do that.'

Eventually, the shopping was over, and they arrived home just as it started to rain quite heavily. It rained for the rest of the afternoon and didn't stop until it was nearly tea time, by which time James was near bursting to run up the garden to see William.

'Don't get wet!' his Mother warned, as he eventually trotted off to meet his friend.

He arrived at the base of the mulberry tree quite breathless. Kneeling down in front of it, called his friend's name and straight away William answered from deep within the tree.

'Make yourself small and come on up.'

Immediately James picked a mulberry leaf, rubbed it between his fingers and wished. In a twinkling of an eye was small enough to make his way inside the tree to where William lived. As he approached his living room he became aware of a brilliant light filling the room with rainbows. As he entered he saw Titania who was the most beautiful creature that he had ever seen. She was taller than William and dressed in gossamer gold that shone like the the sun. She wore a golden crown on her head encrusted with diamonds, rubies and pearls and long diaphanous wings.

As James entered she smiled at him, but James was just lost for words.

'This is James,' said William.

'You are very welcome,' she said. 'William has been telling me how kind you have been to the animals that he looks after and how you are also very brave, so I am going to give you a gift that will help you in your kindly acts.'

Then she reached up into the air and made a circle with her fingers. Suddenly she was holding a small silver box.

'Here you are,' she said. 'Now this is no ordinary box as it contains a powerful magic that will take you anywhere in the world that you want to go, but only if it is used to help someone in need. Always remember James, that as long as you remain true to yourself, honest and loving, you will never be far from the magic of life, but if ever you become selfish or cruel, it all disappears and its joy will turn to bitterness, tears and sadness.'

She passed him the box, and for a little while he could only stand there looking at her in wonder. Then suddenly he felt that he was regaining his proper size.

'Oh thank you, thank you,' he managed to say, as he quickly made his way down the maze of passages into the garden again clutching his precious gift.

No sooner had he arrived than his mother called to tell him that his tea was ready.

'My goodness,' she said, 'you do look pleased with yourself.' James just smiled and tucked into his beans on toast.

Nine

Later that evening James was in his bedroom sitting on the side of his bed looking at the small silver box that Titania had given him and wondering if what the fairy had said was really true. Being full of curiosity, he cautiously opened it and said;

'I wish that I was in Africa.'

Then, to his amazement the box started to grow. A matter of moments later it was almost as big as his bed. Full of excitement, he got inside it and closed the lid.

He could hear the wind as the box sped through the clouds at the speed of light. A few seconds later he felt a bump. Lifting the lid, not knowing what to expect, he was astonished to find himself in the middle of a forest! Monkeys were swinging from the branches of the trees high above him, chattering away to each other.

Getting out of the box, he was fascinated to see it shrink until it was its usual size again.

'My,' he thought, 'is this really happening?'

Then, a family of elephants trundled close by, making him realise that it was very real indeed. He was so excited that he didn't for one moment think that he might be in danger.

Just at that moment he heard a cry for help coming from somewhere nearby. Following the sound, he soon discovered a big hole in the ground not far from where he was standing. Anxious to find out who had fallen in, he made his way cautiously towards it and peeped over the edge.

To his surprise he saw a small boy standing at the bottom, unable to get out.

'It's all right!' called James.

Laying down on his tummy, he tried to reach him, but the little boy was just out of reach.

James stood up and then, to his horror, he saw a snake sliding slowly towards him. Quick as a flash he jumped out of the way and the snake slithered off.

Then he had an idea. Reaching down into the hole with the stick, he told the little boy to catch hold of the end of it, which he did. James pulled and pulled and soon the little boy was safely out of the hole.

He was younger than James and was wearing a bright multi coloured necklace.

'Oh thank you, thank you,' he said. 'I was so frightened. By the way, my name is Jacob. Would you like to come and meet my parents?'

'Oh yes please!' he replied. 'That would be lovely. By the way, my name is James.'

As they walked together the half a mile or so to a clearing at the edge of the forest where a cluster of thatched huts came into view, Jacob told him that he had been playing hide and seek with his friends. Suddenly it had started to rain and became very dark. Then, because he couldn't see where he was going, he had fallen into the pit and couldn't get out. That was where James had found him.

Arriving at the village, they were soon surrounded by Jacob's family and friends. They cheered and clapped because they were, so happy to see him back home safe and well. Everyone of course wanted to hear what had happened to him. Jacob had just finished relating his adventure and telling them how James had rescued him, when James realised that his magic box was starting to become very warm.

He shouted his goodbyes to everybody and quickly ran behind one of the huts and whispered to the box.

'Please take me home.'

In an instant the magic started to work as it again expanded. James then quickly jumped inside and was immediately whisked off to his bedroom. Once out of the box, which quickly became its normal size again, he got into his pyjamas and his mother came into his room to bring up his bedtime glass of milk.

'You've been very quiet,' she said. 'Are you feeling alright?'

'Oh yes mother,' he replied, 'I'm feeling fine.'